# DORA the EXPLORER

# Dora Goes To School

adapted by Leslie Valdes
based on the teleplay by Leslie Valdes
illustrated by Robert Roper

SIMON AND SCHUSTER

Based on the TV series *Dora the Explorer* as seen on Nick Jr.

SIMON AND SCHUSTER
First published in Great Britain in 2005 by Simon & Schuster UK Ltd
1st Floor, 222 Gray's Inn Road, London WC1X 8HB

Originally published in the USA in 2004 by Simon Spotlight,
an imprint of Simon & Schuster Children's Division, New York.

A CIP catalogue record for this book is available from the British Library

ISBN 978-0-85707-422-5

Printed in China

10 9 8 7 6 5 4 3

Visit our websites: www.simonandschuster.co.uk
www.nick.co.uk

¡Hola! I'm Dora and this is my best friend, Boots. It's our first day of school today! And look, there's our teacher, *Maestra Beatriz!* She's on her way to school too.

*Maestra Beatriz* has to get to school before the students do, but her bicycle has just got a flat tyre. We have to help her get to school fast!

First she needs us to help carry her school supplies. Where can we put her supplies? Yeah! Backpack can carry them.

Now let's find the quickest way to school. Who do we ask for help when we don't know which way to go? Map, right!

Map says we need to go through Letter Town, over Number Mountain, and that's the quickest way to get to school. I hear the first school bell. We need to get to school before the third bell. We'd better hurry!

Can you see something that will take us through Letter Town fast? *Sí. El autobus* will take us through the town. *¡Vámonos!*

We need to follow the alphabet along the streets to get through Letter Town. Sing the alphabet with me!

Uh-oh, I hear the second school bell. We really need to hurry! *¡Rápido!* I can see some mountains up ahead. Which one is Number Mountain?

We made it to Number Mountain! Who can give us a ride over it? Our friend Azul the train! *¡Sí!*

To ride over Number Mountain we have to count the numbers. Count with me: 1, 2, 3, 4, 5, 6, 7, 8, 9, 10. That's great!

Now let's count backwards as we ride down the other side: 10, 9, 8, 7, 6, 5, 4, 3, 2, 1. Yay! We made it over Number Mountain.

There's the school! But to get there we need to cross the forest. Here comes my cousin Diego. He says the Condors can fly us over the forest.

Will you help us call the Condors so we can get to school superfast? You need to say "Squawk, squawk!" Say it louder!

Good calling!
Now we can ride the Condors all the way to the school.
You need to hold on tight! Whee!

We made it to school! Now we have to run inside and set up the classroom before the other students come in.

**Will you check Backpack to find *Maestra Beatriz's* school supplies?**

Yay! We found *Maestra Beatriz's* school supplies, but I hear Swiper! That sneaky fox will try to swipe them! We have to say "Swiper, no swiping!" Say it with me: "Swiper, no swiping!"

Thanks for helping us stop Swiper! Look, here come *Maestra Beatriz's* other students.

"Good morning, class!" says *Maestra Beatriz.*

"*¡Buenos dias!*" say the students.

I hear the third school bell! Thanks for helping us get to school on time!